The Murders in the Reed Moore Library

❧ *Chapter 1* ❧

On top of the hill, right above the green swath of lawn where C. Auguste Dupin liked to nap in the sun and watch the humans walk past, sprawled the Reed Moore library. Named, of course, after Reed Moore, the founder of the logging company Moore Wood, who built the long-house library for the town. The library sported massive logs that gleamed golden in the sunshine and a green metal roof. Soaking in the sunshine, the library looked like it enjoyed the warmth as much as a cat. Dupin stretched out a leg and took a long lazy lick off the long white fur on the back of his leg. He rubbed his leg across his face, then repeated the process on the other side.

There. Ready to go inside, just as soon as the librarian, Penny Copper caught up and opened the doors.

As she always did on sunny mornings, Penny had stopped at the fountain to read and eat an apple while Dupin lounged nearby. Sometimes she forgot all about opening the library and Dupin had to rub against her legs to remind her.

Today she remembered on her own and Dupin ran on ahead.

"Slow down!" Penny complained, but laughed.

Dupin sat down. It wasn't as if he hurried. She walked towards him up the concrete sidewalk, a typical enough human although more slender than most, with short blond fur on her head. The rest of her was so bare that, like many humans, she wore clothing. In this case a dark blue skirt, white shirt and a blazer that matched the skirt. As humans went, she looked as neat as a cat, which was saying a great deal. Dupin closed his eyes. He stayed that way until his whiskers picked up the breeze of her passing and the faint scent of apple tickled his nose. Then he opened his eyes and followed along behind.

At the library doors Penny pulled out her brass key ring and stopped. "Would you look at that!"

Dupin curled around her legs and leaned against the back of her calves. It was time to get inside where she kept a can of tuna. Anything else could wait.

Instead, Penny actually walked away from him towards the book drop that crouched beside the doors like a big green toad. Books stuck out of the drop's mouth, and a few had fallen to the ground.

Dupin sat down. The end of his tail twitched.

Penny picked up the fallen books and pulled more out of the mouth of the drop. "If the drop is full, why not bring them back when we're open?"

Dupin closed his eyes. He knew the answer, just as he knew all the answers, but if Penny really wanted to know she'd have to figure it out herself.

Except when he closed his eyes Dupin smelled something almost as interesting as tuna. He opened his mouth slightly and breathed in. Yes, nearby. It smelled almost like a freshly killed field mouse but stronger and greasier. Dupin stood up and followed the scent. It was coming from the book drop where Penny was still pulling out books.

Dupin crouched right beside the metal door in the side. Yes, indeed. Right there, just a small pool of blood had oozed out from inside the drop. Dupin opened his mouth wider and breathed in deep. It made his fur stand on end. This wasn't a field mouse, gopher or bird. It smelled like a person. All sweat and chemicals with an under-scent of fire and smoke.

He backed away from the drop and a growl rumbled in his throat.

"Dupin? What's wrong, silly cat?"

Penny bent down to stroke him, tucking the books she had gathered into one arm, but Dupin flattened his ears and didn't look away from the blood. Finally, she looked at the metal door and saw the blood herself. Her hand went to her mouth.

"Oh!"

She stood up and hurried towards the doors, the keys jangled on the brass key ring, and her shoes made sharp knocking noises against the flagstones.

Dupin followed right on her heels.

Penny unlocked the door and, as soon as it opened a few inches, Dupin darted inside. He immediately felt safer surrounded by the rich smell of the library. He padded quickly across the lobby to the polished cedar service desk, crouched, and sprang right up on top. He turned in a circle surveying the library as Penny followed him inside.

With the hanging lights out shadows draped the library. To Dupin's left was the children's end of the library with the short shelves and a large open area at the center where Penny told stories. On his right the taller adult shelving, comfortable chairs and, under the wing, the computer lab. At a cursory glance all looked as it should but Dupin still had the scent of the blood in his nose, and it kept his fur up. He needed his tuna, and some water, and a good cleaning before he would feel completely calm.

It didn't look like Penny was getting his tuna. She put the books down on the counter next to a computer and picked up the phone instead.

Dupin padded across the counter, hopped over one computer keyboard, and batted at the coiled black phone cord. Penny shook her head and pulled the cord away from him!

That wasn't right. It was too late to do anything about the man — from the smell it had to be a man — in the book drop. But she could still get Dupin his tuna!

"Police?" Penny pressed a hand to her chest. "This is Ms. Copper, at the library? There's blood in my book drop."

Dupin sat down, tail twitching.

"Right. Blood, on the ground from inside. Like something was bleeding." Penny shook her head. "No, I haven't opened it. I was taking out books that were stuck in the slot and Dupin noticed the blood. Yes, my cat. I came inside and called you."

As if they could do anything about the man either, it was too late! Dupin stared at Penny. Tuna? Remember that?

"Yes, thank you. I won't touch it." Penny put down the phone and looked at Dupin. "What could it be? Do you think someone poured blood into the drop? Why would they do that?"

Dupin meowed and stood up. Time to worry about the tuna, and no, the blood hadn't been poured into the drop. Beneath the blood, he smelled the salty, sour smell of a man and a whiff of decay. Someone put a dead man in the book drop as if he was an overdue book. It was too late to do anything about him. The police could handle getting him out. Dupin turned in a circle and looked back at Penny. Tuna!

Penny reached out and scratched his head with one hand. Dupin forced down the purr. Not scratches! Tuna!

"We should look around," Penny announced. "Make sure nothing else looks out of place."

No, not a good idea. Penny walked away from the counter into the back work area, which took her closer to the tuna. Okay, maybe a good idea. Dupin jumped down to the floor and walked quickly after her. He caught up, walked through her legs and headed towards the door to the staff room.

Dupin walked around the workstations at the center of the work area, past the rows of Coroplast boxes full of books along the back wall, into the staff room. Home away from home. Not much of a room with an old green couch marked with his claws, and a wobbly table and two scratched dark wood chairs.

Dupin went to the cupboard where Penny kept the tuna and rubbed against the door. He arched his back and looked back at her.

Penny put her hands on the door frame and leaned into the room. Then she pulled back and walked away, her footsteps muffled by the short carpet.

He couldn't believe it. She left. Without getting the tuna. Dupin stood still in shock. She actually walked away without getting his tuna out. Looking around the library could wait, he couldn't!

Humans! If they didn't have thumbs they'd be no use at all!

Dupin ran after Penny.

He caught up when she flicked on the light in her office. He rubbed against her legs and twitched his tail to catch her attention. Instead she ignored him, looking around the office as if the glass-topped computer desk, or the pictures of Mt. Rainier from her climbs, held some secret. Everything looked as neat as ever, but more importantly, it smelled fine. Dupin circled her legs again.

She sighed and walked away from the office, out of the work area altogether. Dupin was trying to decide what to do about it when Penny screamed! He crouched down and flattened his ears.

Why had she screamed? She was standing just out of the work area, behind the circulation desk. She had her hands pressed to her face now. Dupin rose slightly and opened his mouth. He breathed deep and picked up a faint sticky scent of decay, but mingled with it a floral smell. That wasn't the smell of the man in the book drop.

Dupin padded up beside Penny. There, in the wood book drop beneath the counter, he saw dark red curls, the top of some woman's head. Another dead person in a book drop? What was going on? He smelled salt and looked up to see tears falling from Penny's eyes. She sniffed and wiped her hand on her eyes. She took a deep breath and turned and headed back towards her office, nearly stepping on Dupin. Not that he'd be so slow as to let that happen.

He heard Penny in her office picking up the phone again. More calls to the police. Dupin walked closer to the drop and breathed deep. He didn't smell any blood. The woman didn't die the same way as the man in the outside book drop. Dead people in book drops, that wasn't right. His fur rose up, and he growled deep in his throat. Not right at all. Who hid their kills in a book drop? There had to be better places. Whoever did this put the bodies there for a reason. They wanted the bodies found. Why?

Penny sounded upset, almost yelling into the phone. Dupin walked closer to the drop, but he couldn't see inside. Just the dark red curls sticking up out of the drop. In the office, he heard Penny put down the phone. He went over to the drop and rose up, putting his front paws against the wood. He opened his mouth and breathed in deep.

Death smells, he knew those from killing mice and birds. Stronger from the much larger human. It made him sneeze.

"Dupin!"

He tried to turn, but he had been so focused that Penny was right behind him. She grabbed him before he could twist away and lifted him up into the air. Human thumbs! He didn't fight. He just went limp. She marched across the work area, turned right and then held him just with one hand. She opened the metal door in the back corner and set him outside on the concrete ramp!

Dupin shook himself and started to turn and dart back inside, but at that moment Penny pulled the door closed. Dupin stared at the gray metal in shock.

She put him out! Without his tuna?!

Dupin reached out one paw and drew his claws along the metal. He waited for a second, then did it again. Nothing. Twice more and no response. Annoyed Dupin sat down in front of the door and used both paws, alternating. Scratch, *scratch*, scratch, *scratch*!

Penny didn't come!

Dupin gave out a frustrated yowl and swiped at the door again. She actually put him out without his tuna because of dead bodies? Clearly, she didn't have her priorities in order. Which meant she was going to need his help to put things right. Dupin gave the door a final swipe.

First things, first. How was he going to get back inside?

❧ *Chapter 2* ❧

Sirens screeched through the morning air. Dupin flattened his ears and looked towards the road. Police. He bounded off the concrete path into the dark space beneath the rhododendron bushes. Dried leaves crunched beneath his feet. He padded quickly away from the back door, slipping from one bush to the next. He caught a whiff of a squirrel but didn't stop. Out on the street, the police sirens rang out again and again.

Dupin reached the corner of the building and broke into a trot as the police cars pulled into the parking lot. Uniformed bodies poured out of the cars. Vans pulled behind the cars, and more people got out. So many people! He picked up the pace and made it to the front doors before any of the police or other humans even got close to the building. Dupin crouched beneath the bench along the left side of the walkway, near the black metal bike racks. It smelled of burnt tobacco beneath the bench and one stale bag of chips.

The library's front door swung open. Penny's shoes shuffled on the concrete as she edged away from the book drop. Dupin darted out from his place of concealment, like the shadow of a bird he flew across the concrete for the narrow open gap.

"Dupin!"

He sensed rather than saw her reach for him but she was far too slow. By then he'd already entered the library. He headed at first towards the counter area, but that's where the other body was in the other book drop. He swerved and headed instead towards the heavy padded chairs and one of his favorite spots beneath. Enclosed on three sides, but with an opening beneath the back, he liked watching people come and go in the library.

Safe in the shadows beneath the chair Dupin, surrounded by his own scent markings, settled down and watched Penny at the door with the police. Another scent distracted him. Dupin sniffed around and found an envelope beneath the chair that smelled of mint. He rubbed his face against it, one side, then the other. Out by the lobby, the police crowded around Penny but she didn't cringe or back away from them. She stood right up to the man who was in charge.

That man wore a long black coat that reminded Dupin of ravens. He tried to get some raven chicks once. Actually went so far as to climb the tree after the nest but the parents saw him and chased him away. Even after he was on the ground, they had kept coming after him with their harsh cries and nasty beaks. Dupin narrowed his eyes, wondering if that man was like the ravens.

Penny led the police into the library right towards Dupin's hiding place. He shrank back a bit further into the shadows. Penny's hand waved at the counter.

"The other one is over there, in the bin."

The man in the black coat stood close to Penny. Dupin could smell a fishy sort of smell about the man from where he was hiding. It made him feel a little better about the man but reminded him that he still hadn't got his tuna. Even so, he stayed concealed.

"Ms. Copper, you said the door was locked when you entered the library?"

"I thought so. I didn't check before I put the key in and turned it to open the door. I always do it that way, the door stays locked until you flip the little switch on the door."

"So it was possible that it wasn't locked?"

"I guess so, although I always double-check the locks when I leave."

Dupin eased forward a bit. That man was writing something in a notebook. Abruptly he looked down past his pad and fixed blue eyes on Dupin.

Dupin froze in place, staring back at the man.

The man pointed a pencil at Dupin. "That your cat?"

"Yes, detective Clemm. I can't understand why anyone would do this? Kill someone and put them here?"

The detective blinked first. Dupin yawned widely just so the detective got a good look at his fangs.

"Call me David, Ms. Copper. It's too early to speculate. When did you last close up?"

"Saturday. Four p.m., our usual time."

"And were you the last to leave?"

"No. Henry was with me. And Dupin, of course. We don't like to have people leave alone, even if it isn't dark. Just to be safe. We walked out together. I pulled on the doors to make sure that they were locked. I know I did."

"Okay, and this Henry can confirm that? A last name?"

"Yes. Duvall."

"Who has access to the building?"

"It's a city-owned building, it was donated when the library was built. You'd know better than me who has access over there. All of my staff have keys. The city hires cleaning staff, so they must have keys too because they get in and clean the library after hours."

Dupin eased out of the space beneath the chair. He walked over to Penny and rubbed against her legs. He let a low purr rumble through his chest.

Penny's legs stayed anchored as if she had grown out of the floor.

"Do you have any enemies? Anyone with something against you? Or the library?"

Penny? Hardly. Dupin observed lots of humans, and he knew better than most that everyone loved Penny. He'd even go so far as forgiving her for forgetting his tuna. Eventually. Bored, Dupin wandered away from Penny towards the circulation desk.

Teams of people had gathered around the desk while the detective talked to Penny. They had pulled the book return bin out from the desk. Dupin padded closer, edging around the end of the desk. He sat down beside one of the tall pillars where he could watch and still keep an eye on Penny. Just in case she decided to get his tuna.

They were all so busy about the dead people, it was like someone had stirred up a nest of yellow jackets. Another cluster of people buzzed around the book drop outside. They had that one open too and had pulled the bin partway out before it got stuck on books that had piled on top of the body.

"We'll have more questions later," the detective said.

"Can I go back to my office?" Penny asked. "I should call our staff and tell them we won't be opening today."

The detective shook his head. "Please stay here, until my people have a chance to look everything over." Blue eyes found Dupin sitting beside the pillar. "If you could keep the cat out of our way, that'd be good too."

Out of the way? Dupin closed his eyes just to show the man how important he was.

He heard Penny's footsteps approaching and looked up. Penny got close, and Dupin let out a small meow. He arched his back, expecting a scratch but she scooped him up into her arms instead. She brought him close to her chest and wrapped her arms around him. For a second Dupin tensed, then he relaxed and breathed in her apple scent. No tuna. Yet.

Penny carried him away before he could see anything interesting, including the dead body. She took him back to the stuffed chairs and sat in the one he had hidden beneath. She absently stroked his back. Dupin flexed his claws and stretched out first his left leg, then his right. He put his head down and closed his eyes. If he couldn't eat, he might as well sleep.

As he drifted off to sleep, he heard Penny talking on her cell phone. He didn't like her being sad, so he purred loudly as he drifted off.

Dupin found himself rudely woken when Penny stood up and put him down on the floor. He shook himself and took a couple stiff steps away before he stopped to clean the nap from his fur.

"Thank you, detective." Penny rubbed her arms. "Did you find anything? Who are those people?"

David reached out and put a hand on Penny's arm. "I thought you might be able to help us with that. You get a lot of people in here, do you feel up to taking a look? See if you recognize them? They don't have any identification on them."

Dupin paused in his cleaning and looked at Penny. If she could lay her ears back or have her fur stand up, he thought she would do so. She took a deep breath and nodded.

"Yes. Of course, if it will help."

David stepped close. "I'll be right there with you. There's something else?"

"Yes?"

"The books in the outside drop, can you tell who checked those out?"

Penny shivered. "Yes, but I'd need a subpoena to release those records. They're confidential under state law. Why do you want to know who checked out the books?"

"A lot of the books we removed had fallen on the body. Others were beneath the body. Anyone returning books might have seen something suspicious or someone hanging around."

"Makes sense, I'll just need you to get a subpoena."

David grinned. "Of course."

"And I'll need the books."

He shook his head. "We've taken the books to examine for evidence. I can get you the barcode numbers."

"That'd be fine."

This all was about as interesting to Dupin as getting his nails trimmed. He stretched out his legs and took a long stretch with a satisfying yawn.

"If you're ready?" David asked, gesturing towards the lobby where the two bodies waited on gurneys.

Penny crossed her arms but nodded. Figuring the most likely possibility of tuna lay in sticking close to Penny, Dupin followed along after Penny and David into the lobby. There lay the dead man and woman in black body bags upon the gurney, with all of the assorted smells of death.

David unzipped the first bag. "Do you recognize him?"

Dupin looked over at Penny. She nodded. "That's Bill Wilson. He teaches over at the high school. Who would want to kill him?"

"That's what we need to find out." David zipped up the dead man's bag and then moved around to the other one. He unzipped it. "Her?"

Penny didn't move from the spot where she stood. She stared for several seconds then took a deep shuddering breath. "Camille. Camille L'Espanye. She works here at the library." Penny brought her hand to her mouth and sniffed. "Camille? Why?"

Dupin stood up and looked at the body bag with more interest. He breathed deep and, yes, Penny was correct. The woman was Camille. She gave him extra cat treats when Penny wasn't looking. And now she was dead too? His fur stood up.

"She had keys to the building," David said. "Maybe she came back for something and interrupted whatever was happening with Mr. Wilson. Or maybe they were together? Do you know if they were dating?"

Penny shook her head. "Camille's ten years younger than him. She's just out of college. I don't think she was seeing anyone seriously."

David made notes in his book. "We'll check on it anyway. Thank you, Ms. Copper. If I have more questions, I'll let you know."

The detective zipped up the bag and motioned to the people waiting outside. Two men in blue suits came and took away the gurneys. Dupin meowed softly.

Camille dead. That disturbed him. Bad enough he hadn't gotten his tuna and Penny was upset, but killing Camilla? Dupin's eyes narrowed. He wasn't going to wait around for David to try and figure it out. The man seemed well-meaning enough, but he was hampered by being human. His only advantage was the fact of his thumbs but that didn't matter.

Dupin looked up at Penny quietly crying. He had his own human, with her own set of thumbs. She wasn't a cat, but for a human she seemed quite bright. Between the two of them, he felt confident in their ability to find the responsible party.

And then maybe she'd remember to get him his tuna!

ॐ *Chapter 4* ॐ

Dupin watched the gurneys being wheeled down the sidewalk to the waiting ambulances before he turned his attention back to Penny, standing beside him with tears running down her cheeks.

No tuna. Penny upset. Camille and that teacher, Bill Wilson, dead. Someone had to pay for their crimes, and Dupin didn't trust David to figure out what happened. No, it'd be better for all concerned if Dupin and Penny identified the criminal.

First, he needed Penny to get curious.

He knew his human. She loved finding answers. He watched her each day in the library answering questions for the people that came in and out. While her intellect might not match his own — that would no doubt be impossible for a human — she still showed almost cat-like insight. And she had thumbs, the one human attribute that saved the entire species.

David came back inside. "You'll be staying here?"

Penny nodded. "Is that okay? Are you done with—?"

"Yes. We're done. I'm releasing the scene. I can send in a couple officers to help clean up if you like?"

Dupin meowed and bumped against her legs. He didn't want any more humans tromping all over.

Penny shook her head. "We'll be okay. I'll take care of it. I've got to clean things up. We won't be opening today."

David nodded. "Okay then. I'll get that subpoena for the checkout records and stop by later?"

"Okay. I'll need the barcode list, too."

"I'll have it for you." David turned and left.

Penny looked down at Dupin. "It's just you and me now."

Just the way he liked it. Dupin rubbed

against her legs. Penny stepped around him. "Let's go clean up, then."

Dupin ran between Penny's legs into the library. The library smelled of latex gloves and fingerprint powders. He sneezed and stalked closer to the circulation counter. When he got there, he padded across the top towards an area covered in fingerprint dust.

"Dupin!" Penny rushed up to the counter and put a hand out in his path. "Don't walk in that! That's all we need, are cat prints tracked all over."

As if he wanted to track that stuff all over and get it in his fur? Dupin sat down and licked one paw to prove his point. Penny put her hands on her hips and sniffled. "It's just so —"

A bright reflection beneath the keyboard caught Dupin's eye. Ignoring the powder, he walked through it to the keyboard and fished beneath with his claws.

"Dupin! You're getting dirty!"

He ignored her and tried to get his claws into whatever it was beneath the keyboard. Not for the first time he considered the intangible mystery of why cats didn't have thumbs. His claw hooked onto a metal ring, and he dragged out a small brass key hooked to a red plastic tab by the ring on his claw. He shook his paw, and the key clattered in the fingerprint dust. Dupin slammed a paw down on the rattling key.

"What's that?" Penny asked. She reached out, and Dupin drew back his paw.

She picked it up neatly, pinching the small ring between a finger and her thumb. "What's the book drop key doing here?"

Confident in her ability to answer that for herself, Dupin jumped down from the counter and sniffed around the book bin that had held Camille. The police had gone over the wood bin, but they didn't have the benefit of a cat's nose. The bin still smelled of death. It needed cleaning.

Penny lifted the key up in front of her face. "It looks like a fingerprint, in the dust on the plastic tab." She lowered it to the counter and set it down. "We'll have to show that to David when he comes back."

Maybe so, but it didn't answer any questions right now. Dupin left the bin and sat down to clean the fingerprint powder off his paws. It tasted like ashes and made him sneeze.

"Oh, you poor kitty," Penny said. "Stop licking it! Let me get a rag, and we'll get this all cleaned up."

Dupin didn't bother stopping. Penny left the counter area and headed back into the staff room. Dupin realized that this put Penny near the tuna and took off running after her. Unfortunately, he realized too late and she surprised him in the doorway holding wet paper towels. Dupin tried slipping around her, but Penny caught him. She grabbed his feet and rubbed them with the wet towels. It was almost as bad as being licked by a dog! She finally released him, and he headed under the nearby desk where he sat cleaning his drenched paws.

While he cleaned himself, Penny busied herself cleaning the counter area, except for the spot where she left the key. She used a spray on the book drop, the sort that made his eyes water, so he stayed back beneath the desk and just watched. Penny noticed the scratch along the side of the bin.

"What happened —?" She sniffled. "Oh."

Dupin rose and strolled out from under the desk as Penny finished cleaning the bin and pushed it back beneath the counter. She looked at Dupin.

"Why would anyone kill Camille?"

Dupin meowed.

Penny smiled. "Okay. You're right. I should be trying to find out something to help David with his case. Like why Camille might have been here. Or why anyone would kill Bill Wilson. I always thought he seemed nice enough. He thought he was more charming than he was, but a lot of men are like that."

Dupin jumped up on the desk and sniffed at the papers there. A red file folder sitting on the desk smelled like Camille. He pushed it with his paw towards the edge of the desk.

"Dupin!" Penny ran over and caught the folder before it fell. "You're acting so strange. Do you miss her too?"

At least he missed the extra treats. People came and went in his life, always had until Penny.

Penny flipped through the folder. "These are Camille's! How did you know?"

Didn't they smell like Camille? It should be obvious, but Penny suffered from the same poor sense of smell as most humans.

Dupin arched his back for a scratch, but Penny didn't notice.

"The deadline for these financial aid forms is today." Penny looked at Dupin. "This could be very helpful. If she left these forms here, it could explain why she came back to the library last night."

Penny carried folder towards the front desk. Dupin jumped off the desk and followed her to the counter. She put the folder down next to the key. Dupin jumped up on the counter. From the counter, it was much easier to look at Penny's face.

He meowed and arched his back again. Penny reached out and stroked his fur. "Good kitty."

Dupin purred happily against her hand. He still wanted his tuna, but scratches were progress. Except then Penny stopped. She tapped her fingers on the counter.

"So Camille comes back to the library to get the folder she forgot. I still don't see how that ties in with Bill Wilson. I can't imagine they were involved."

Dupin sat down and waited.

Penny crossed her arms and stared at the book drop key for several seconds. Then she glanced over at the cleansers she had used on the wood book drop bin.

"I should check the outside drop, make sure it's been cleaned up before anyone puts more books in it." Penny pulled open a drawer on the back of the counter and rummaged in a plastic basket with a good dozen keys, each attached to a bright plastic tag. Dupin yawned. Penny took out another key, a duplicate of the one sitting in that small patch of fingerprint dust.

Penny tossed it in the air and caught it. "Let's do that."

She tucked the spray bottle and a roll of paper towels beneath her arm before heading towards the outside doors. Dupin followed. Before they got to the lobby, Penny stopped. Dupin came up from behind and rubbed against her leg and then stopped too. Several people were standing outside the main doors. Penny took a breath and then started walking again.

Dupin trotted along after. Penny went out to the main doors and pushed them open a crack. Four humans stood outside. A man smelling of sawdust with red cheeks and dark hair stepped forward.

"We saw the police. What was going on?"

The other humans, a red-haired woman, and an older couple came closer. Dupin sat down just behind Penny where he could see everyone. He breathed in deeply. The woman smelled of fire and smoke. It reminded him of the body that had been in the bin, but much stronger. The older couple had smelled almost the same as each other, a dry, powdery, minty sort of old smell like dried leaves.

Penny took a deep breath. "Two people were killed. The library won't be opening today, I'm sorry."

"Killed?" The old woman gasped and looked up at her husband. He put an arm around her. "That's awful!"

The red-haired woman stepped closer. Dupin watched her warily.

"Look, I've just got to pick up something for my class. It'll only take a second," the woman said.

Penny shook her head. "We're not opening today."

The woman moved her hand in a circle as she said, "Look, this is terrible, really. But you know life does go on. Everyone else still has places to go, things to do, and

I don't mean to be a bitch, but Camille said my book was supposed to be in last week and it didn't come in which meant I lost the whole weekend. Then I get this email saying it's there and I just need to pick it up. You don't even have to do anything, I'll grab it and check it out."

Penny shook her head. "I can't let you in right now. If —"

"Look, how hard is it —"

"If you'll just tell me your name, I'll get the book."

The red-haired woman stared at Penny for a second then shook her head. "Look, just forget it. I don't have time for this."

The woman turned and left. Her heels made rapid clicks against the sidewalk as she walked quickly away. Dupin watched her go.

Then the man standing beside Penny shook his head. "Guess she didn't need it that much after all." He held out his hand. "Rod Allan."

"I guess not." Penny shook his hand and let go quickly. "Folks, I'm sorry, but we won't be open today. If you'll excuse me, I need to clean the drop."

"Can I help?" Rod asked.

The old couple started to move away, but the old man pulled free from his wife's arm. Both Penny and the man looked up as the older man approached. He had pale blue eyes and very pale saggy skin.

"Lo! Death has reared himself a throne," he said. "In a strange city lying alone —"

His wife tugged on his arm. "Come on Sullivan." She looked at Penny. "He likes quoting. That's about all he can remember these days, are poems and lines from plays."

"It's fine." Penny looked at Rod. "I can take care of this myself. Please, I'd prefer to be alone."

Dupin watched the old couple move off, the woman tugging on the man's arm. Rod moved away a couple steps and rubbed his rough jaw. Dupin waited to see what he intended to say when a police car rolled up in front of the library. Rod ducked his head, stuffed his hands in his pockets and walked away down the sidewalk.

David got out of the police car. He walked past Rod and headed straight towards Penny. Dupin got up and strolled over to Penny. He rubbed against her legs.

"Hello," Penny said when David reached them.

"Hello again, yourself." He reached into his jacket and pulled out a few sheets of paper. "I've got the subpoena and the barcode list. Are you ready to help me out now?"

Penny took the paper and looked it over. "This looks fine. You just need to know who had these checked out?"

"And any contact information you have. We'll need to question them."

Penny nodded. "In this case, I don't see that we have any choice if it'll help catch the killer."

"It might." David opened the library door. "Shall we?"

"I was going to clean the drop."

"I'm sure my people cleaned it after they were done."

"I don't know about that," Penny shook her head. "They left a mess inside."

Dupin meowed.

"See? Dupin agrees."

David chuckled. "Okay. If Dupin agrees, I stand corrected."

Penny held up a finger. "It'll only take

a minute, and I'll feel better. Then I've got something to show you inside."

"Okay."

Penny unlocked the book drop, twisted the handle and pulled open the metal door. Dupin peered around into the drop. It still smelled of the dead man, Bill Wilson. Penny reached inside and pulled the bin out. Dupin moved aside, and once the drop was out of the way, he went to the opening and looked into the drop. A dark flat shape lay against the side of the drop.

Dupin strolled inside. He went to the thing he had seen and sniffed. It turned out to be a leather wallet that smelled like the dead man. From outside he caught a whiff of the cleansers Penny sprayed on the drop.

He pawed at the wallet. It fell open. There were pictures inside. Dupin took a long look. Penny needed to see this. He meowed and crouched as the drop magnified and echoed the sound.

Chapter 5

Dupin turned his head smoothly and looked at the bright opening of the book drop. Two human faces looked in at him. Penny on the right, smiling and on the left the blue-eyed gaze of David. Dupin crouched down and kept his paw on the wallet.

"What is that?" David asked.

"It looks like a wallet. Just a sec." Penny crouched and walked into the drop bent over. Dupin backed off the wallet when she reached for it. "Good kitty."

Penny picked up the wallet and waddled back out. For once she lacked her usual cat-like grace. Dupin wouldn't hold it against her. He followed her out of the drop. Penny straightened and flipped the wallet open.

"It's Bill Wilson's."

David fished in his pocket and pulled out a bag. "I'll need to take that."

"Wait a sec," Penny said.

Dupin couldn't see anything. Very frustrating. He looked around and then jumped up on top of the book drop. He walked to the edge and could finally see what Penny was looking at.

Pictures, in the wallet, of the dead man and a young woman with long blond hair. Lots of it, like a Persian cat he'd known once. Penny flipped to the next picture, and it was a picture of the red-haired woman smelling of fire and smoke that had been here just a few minutes ago. Penny held the wallet out to David

"Look at this. She was here earlier, but who is the girl in this picture? Their daughter?"

David made a whistling sound. "If that's his wife, what was she doing here? Did she say anything about her husband?"

Penny shook her head. "She just wanted to pick up a book."

"You didn't tell her?" David asked.

"No, I didn't know who she was. Haven't you already contacted the families?"

"Not her. We haven't been able to get a hold of her." David flipped back to the first photo. "But that girl isn't their daughter. They don't have a daughter. We already checked with the school."

"Oh."

David dropped the wallet into the baggy. "This might just be the clue we needed. Thanks!"

Penny shook her head. She reached out and scratched under Dupin's chin. He closed his eyes with pleasure. "It was Dupin that found the wallet."

David coughed. "Yes, I guess so. We've got some barcodes to look at?"

First Penny wanted to clean out the book drop bin before she put it back inside. Dupin stretched out on the warm metal drop and snoozed while she worked. When she finished, he jumped down and inside first, as soon as she opened the door. Dupin stopped and looked back, but the humans were moving so slowly. Penny laughed at something David had said.

Dupin recognized the signs of human

courtship. Penny had, on occasion, dated various men. None of whom were good enough for her, a fact that she had quickly realized when Dupin had made his displeasure known.

Penny walked quickly across the library. So quickly that Dupin barely avoided being trodden upon, escaping at the last moment by springing up onto the circulation counter once more. David followed at a more leisurely pace. Penny turned around, facing him with her hands resting on the counter behind her.

"I've got it!" Penny announced.

Dupin walked up behind her and rose up, rubbing the side of his face against her shoulder.

"What have you got?" David asked.

"I know who committed these crimes." Penny's voice turned colder. "I know who killed Camille."

David tapped the list on his hand. "How could you possibly have figured it out?"

Penny shrugged. Dupin rubbed against her other shoulder. Then he sat down and stared at David.

"Well, if the red-head was Mr. Wilson's

wife and the girl in the other picture wasn't, she must have killed them both. Jealous rage, over the affair."

David shook his head. "That might be the case, but we don't have any evidence of that."

"Maybe we do?" Penny turned and gestured at the key sitting on its island of fingerprint dust and Camille's binder. "I thought you might want to look at these. Dupin found key beneath one of the keyboards. It's to the book drop outside."

"Okay, we shouldn't have missed that, but go on."

"We also found Camille's folder with her financial aid forms that needed to be filed today. I think she came back to get the forms. While she was here, she decided to empty the book drop and got in the middle of Mrs. Wilson killing Mr. Wilson! Mrs. Wilson came back today because she realized that she had left this key and was afraid it would lead back to her."

"We haven't established that Mrs. Wilson was here, and why wouldn't she have waited until her husband left the library? Why kill him and Camille?"

Penny frowned. "I don't know. Maybe she

didn't think it through. Maybe she assumed that Camille was also sleeping with her husband."

"I'm not ready to discount anything."

Dupin rubbed against Penny's arm. It was a good idea, but David had a point. Thumbs and the ability to speak that'd make all of this much easier. So would tuna. He walked to the edge of the counter and meowed.

Penny shook her head. "Not now, Dupin."

David lifted the paper. "Let's take this one step at a time. Could you get me the list of people I need?"

"Do you want to wait while I pull it up?"

David shook his head. "No, thanks. It may not pan out, but I do need to talk to Mrs. Wilson before she finds out about her husband from someone else. Just email me the list, my card is there."

"Oh, okay."

"I'll take the key and have it tested. And the folder." David pulled a couple more bags from his pockets. He bagged the key in a small baggy and then the folders in a larger one. "If you find anything else just leave it where you find it and give the department a call. Believe it or not, we'll figure this out."

Dupin crouched and stared at David, his tail flicking back and forth. David noticed and edged back. "Thank you, Ms. Copper."

As David left, Dupin got up and rubbed Penny's arm again. She turned around and scratched his neck, then ran her hand down his back through his long fur. Almost as good as tuna, but he couldn't quite forget the empty knot in his belly.

"I'm going to figure this out," Penny said. "For Camille."

Penny went into her office. Dupin followed and crawled into his bed beneath her desk. While she typed on the computer, he busied himself cleaning his fur again.

It took longer than Dupin thought was possible. Twice he woke from short naps when the drone of the keyboard keys ceased, but each time Penny started typing again. On the third time, she pushed her chair back from the desk. Dupin lifted his head and yawned.

Penny peeked beneath the desk at him. "I've finished the list. It's very interesting."

Of course. Dupin stretched out his legs and did a deep backbend.

"David identified the books that were

underneath Mr. Wilson and those on top of him. They kept track of the layers of books, so we have an idea of when books were put in, in what order. There's not a lot of names on the list."

Dupin stretched his back legs out. She must have a point with all of this.

"That guy from earlier? Rod Allan? He turned in books that were beneath Bill Wilson. There was also a book checked out to Mr. Wilson. And that older couple, they came by yesterday too. I recognized the names when I saw it. Sullivan and Madeline Winters, they returned books that were right on top of the body."

Dupin walked out from under the desk. Interesting. And all of them showed up the next morning? Maybe because one of them wanted to return for their kill? Did humans eat things they killed? They must because they had things like tuna. Dupin's stomach rumbled. He really needed to eat something.

"I'm going to call David, tell him I've emailed the list. He needs to know who came by today." Penny picked up her cell phone and dialed quickly. She leaned back in the chair.

Dupin jumped up onto her lap so that he could hear the conversation better.

"David."

"It's Penny Copper. I just emailed the list you wanted."

"Great, thanks."

"You need to know, the man whose books were right beneath the body, Rod Allan, he came by earlier today. He was here when Bill Wilson's wife was here."

"Really?" Dupin heard the excitement in David's voice even with the phone pressed up against Penny's head.

"And there was an older couple today, the Winters. They had returned books that were on top of the body."

"They're regulars?"

"Yes. I recognized them. I didn't place their names until I saw the list, but yeah, they're in most days."

"Good work. You said the other guy was Rod Allan?"

"Yes? Does that mean something? He offered to help clean the drop."

"Really? Well, that's interesting. We just found out that the picture in Wilson's wallet, of him and the girl? That's Lenore Allan. She's a student in Wilson's class."

Penny ran a hand along Dupin's back. "So he might have gone after Mr. Wilson because of his daughter. That sounds like a motive to me."

"And with his books right beneath the body, he might as well have signed a confession. I love it when cases solve themselves!"

Dupin felt water drip on his ear. He flicked it and looked up at Penny. Water flowed from her eyes. As much as he didn't care for the water, he knew her well enough to know what she was thinking. It was Camille. If this man killed Bill Wilson, then he must have killed Camille just because she saw something. If she hadn't gone back for her folder, she would have been fine.

"Thank you, Ms. Copper. We'll —"

"Penny, please."

"Okay. Penny. Thank you. I think I need to go have a chat with this Allan fellow."

"Alright, bye." Penny hung up the cell phone and put it down on the arm of the couch. Dupin batted at it. Penny snatched it away and stuffed it in her pocket. "Stop that, you're always redialing people. "

Penny pulled a tissue from the green Kleenex box on her desk and dried her tears. She tossed it into the plastic wastebasket beside the desk.

Penny stroked Dupin's back. "Looks like we've solved the crime. Thanks to you. You found the folder and the wallet. Plus that key! And all without your tuna."

Dupin jumped down to the floor and turned in a circle. He meowed. Penny laughed and stood up. "Okay, okay! I'm sorry. It hasn't been a typical day."

Chapter 6

The library phone range while Dupin was in the middle of his after-eating. Penny picked up the extension on the end table beside the couch.

"Reed Moore Library, Penny. How may I help you?" Dupin noticed the change in her expression and paused in his cleaning. He couldn't quite make out the voice on the other end.

"So he didn't do it?" Penny asked after a moment. "But what about the picture?"

Dupin got up and padded over to the couch. He jumped up beside Penny and bumped her arm holding the phone.

Dupin heard David's voice. "— pretty upset about it, but his alibi checked out.

He was giving a business presentation at the time the murders happened. You don't have any way to determine when he dropped the books in the drop, do you?"

"No. His books were just beneath the body."

"Could he have hired someone to do it?"

"Maybe, we'll check into it, but either he's an excellent actor, or he was surprised about that picture."

"What about the wife?" Penny asked.

"She checked out too. Fell apart when we told her, was also shocked by the photo. She's been taking evening classes, and we've confirmed she was in class that night." David was quiet for a minute. "At this point, we don't have much. We got a fingerprint off the key you found, but I'm waiting for search results. Forensics are starting to come in, but it's starting to look like there might have been more than one assailant. Sorry I don't have more."

"That's okay. Thanks for letting me know." Penny hung up the phone. She stroked Dupin. "I guess we didn't solve it after all."

Penny picked Dupin up in her arms and stood. She kept stroking his back, so he didn't mind. "He said there might have been two people. That makes sense. Camille and Mr. Wilson died differently. The key might turn up a match, but what if it didn't?"

He'd already gotten his tuna. As far as he was concerned David was welcome to figure out what really happened. He lay slack in Penny's arms as she walked out of the staff room. She carried him back to the counter and put him down on top. She pressed her hands together. "Okay, Dupin, let's work through this. Camille comes back to the library to pick up her folder. She decides – because she was like that – to go ahead and empty the book drop while she was here. She goes out to empty the drop, and Bill Wilson is still out there. One person stabs him while the other goes after Camille. She tries to get away or call for help by coming in the library. The killer outside shoves the dying Mr. Wilson into the book bin and then pushes it into the book drop, closes and locks the drop. Their partner strangles poor Camille inside and lets the other in, who tosses the key on the counter where it slides beneath the keyboard. They put Camille in the drop in here and then leave."

It made sense, but Dupin's eye noticed something beneath one of the padded chairs. He jumped down from the counter and walked over to the chair. He crouched down and inhaled. The minty-smelling letter still lay where he left it. Dupin reached in and scratched at it. He managed to pull the envelope partway out.

Penny stooped down and picked it up. Dupin rubbed against her legs. Penny's breath caught. She stood very still for several seconds then looked down at Dupin. "Do you know what this is?"

He had a pretty good idea.

"I recognized the Winters, they come in all the time." Penny blew out her breath. "And she's always checking out those serial killer books, from the 364s. This letter is addressed to them. They must have dropped it! What if they're serial killers, working together? They could have dropped the letter when they —"

Penny slid the letter into her pocket and started walking towards the door. "Come on, Dupin. We're going to go talk to them!"

Dupin didn't move. Somehow the idea of talking to a pair of potential killers didn't have much appeal. Plus he'd just eaten all of that tuna, and it sat like a lump in his belly. A nap was the order of the moment. A long nap to allow the tuna time to digest.

"Dupin?" Penny stopped in the doorway. "Here, kitty. Come on. There's nothing to worry about. We'll just be helping David out, see what they say when I ask if they saw anything. Maybe they'll let something slip."

Dupin yawned.

Penny marched towards him. He thought of dashing away, but he hated running on a full stomach. Penny scooped him up and held him close. She pressed her face to his back, and he smelled the apples in her hair.

"I need you with me," she said. "Come on."

Chapter 7

Dupin rolled on his back in the seat beside Penny and tried to bat at the phone again. She moved it away.

"We're almost there now," Penny said.

David was on the phone. "Wait for me. My people can look at the letter. We found hair on the inside drop, and I have people checking the fingerprints on the books against the book drop key. We'll get them."

Penny didn't answer as she turned the steering wheel and slowed. Dupin rolled over and stood up. "I'm on the street now. I need to know why they did it."

"Damn it! Wait! I'll be there soon, and I'll handle it."

The car slowed. "Too late."

"Don't hang up," David said. "At least stay on the line."

Penny slipped the phone into her pocket without saying anything.

The house was set back from the road with fir trees and bird feeders along the fence line. Penny stopped the car. Small brown birds flitted around the tree branches. Dupin perked up his ears. The house itself looked like a lot of human dwellings, yellow and white, mostly uninteresting. The old couple was out front in the yard, the woman pruning rose bushes with a pair of snips and her husband digging in another flower bed with a trowel when Penny lifted Dupin out of the front seat and carried him up the cracked concrete walk.

"Sully?" The old woman called. "Look who it is?"

The old man looked back and squinted so much that only one pale blue eye stayed open. Against his side, Dupin felt Penny's heart thumping away like a mouse caught beneath his paws. She was scared, but she marched straight up the drive towards them. She stopped across the chain-link fence from the woman.

"Mrs. Winters?"

"Call me Maddy, dear. Don't mind my Sully, he's grumpy as usual." The old woman looked at Dupin and smiled broadly. "You'd better keep a good grip on that cat. Wouldn't want him to go after a bird or something and get squashed by a car!"

Penny's arms tightened. "No. I'm helping the police with the murders at the library, and I thought maybe you could tell me something?"

"Murders." Maddy pressed her hands together, and her smile widened to show bright teeth. Dupin didn't like the way she looked at him. "Why would you think we know anything about those poor people?"

"Books you returned were on the body." Dupin felt Penny take a deep breath. "The police took a fingerprint from the books and matched it to the one on the book drop key. They've also found your hair in the inside book drop where you stuffed Camille."

Dupin blinked. That wasn't exactly what David had said. He tensed. If the old woman tried anything, she'd find out how sharp his claws were.

Penny pulled out the letter. "And if that's

not enough, you dropped this when you murdered Camille!"

Maddy stared at Penny for several seconds then chuckled. "Sully? You'd better come here. We've got a bit of a problem."

Penny took a step back. "Why? Why did you do it?"

At the other flower bed, Sully rose and came towards them with his dirt-covered trowel. Maddy snipped her pruning snips closed. "Opportunity. We walked to the library to return books, and there was that man talking to that young girl. No one was around." She opened the snips and snapped them shut again. "As far as motive, well dear, it was our anniversary and we always try to do something special."

Sully had nearly reached the gate. Penny backed away towards the car. Dupin's fur stood up, and he growled deep in his throat. Maddy laughed.

"Run, if you like, but if you're here, the police haven't linked any of that evidence to us. Not yet, at least. We'll disappear and find you another time, dear."

Sully leered at Penny. "By a route obscure and lonely, haunted by ill angels only."

Penny shoved the letter back into her pocket and pulled out the cell phone. Dupin heard the sirens coming towards them. Penny said, "Detective? Did you hear all that?"

"Yes, Ms. Copper." Dupin heard David's voice coming from two directions and turned to see the detective step around the trees along the front into the driveway. He had a gun in his hand. "Mr. and Mrs. Winters put the tools down and come out here with your hands up."

Penny slipped her phone into her pocket and moved back over to her car as David walked up, and several squad cars pulled up in front of the drive.

"I'm glad you called, but you should have waited. We'll confirm the evidence, but with her confession, that'll be icing."

Penny shook her head. "I didn't call. Dupin stepped on the phone in the car. He redialed the last number."

"Huh, his timing couldn't be better if he did it on purpose." David held out his hand. "And I'll need that letter as well as a statement on finding it."

"Dupin found it. I think he figured it all out before any of us."

Officers came up and took the couple into custody. Dupin purred against Penny's chest. Of course, he figured it out first, and why would David think he hadn't made the call on purpose? Nevermore would this couple kill.

❧ *Next* ❧

C. Auguste Dupin returns in *The Task of Auntie Dido*.

Visit ryanwriter.link/poeville

If you want to see more books in this series, you can show your support in several ways:

• Sign up for **Readinary**, my readers' group at ryanmwilliams.com. You'll get updates, news, special deals, and can always unsubscribe.

• Leave a **review** on your favorite review or retail site. Reviews make a big difference for writers. Only a small percentage of readers take time to leave reviews, so it is very much appreciated.

• Like treats, **share** your love of the

story with your friends that will enjoy it. Gift it, tell people about it, cuddle up and read it together!

www.ingramcontent.com/pod-product-compliance
Lightning Source LLC
Chambersburg PA
CBHW032052180726
48284CB00004B/1298

The Murders in the Reed Moore Library

Ryan M. Williams

GLITTERING THRONG PRESS • RAINIER

The Murders in the Reed Moore Library

GTP Book Collectors Number: 1

Printed in the United States of America

First Printing: March 2018

Glittering Throng Press
PO Box 179, Rainier, WA 98576-0179

glitteringthrongpress.com

eBook: 978-1-946440-02-0
Paperback: 978-1-946440-21-1
Hardcover: 978-1-946440-22-8
Large Print: 978-1-946440-23-5

For all my fellow librarians